Bedrooms

Five Comedies

by
Renée Taylor
and
Joseph Bologna

A SAMUEL FRENCH ACTING EDITION

SAMUEL FRENCH

FOUNDED 1830

New York Hollywood London Toronto

SAMUELFRENCH.COM

DAVID AND NANCY

DAVID AND NANCY

The lights fade up on a small bedroom in a middle-class suburban house. It's decorated femininely and tastefully. There is a window in the center of the stage left wall. Next to the window and down stage of it is a desk, chair and bookcase dressed befittingly for a recently-graduated college student. There is a small dressing table and stool against the stage right wall. A single bed is against the upstage wall in the center. Just right of the bed in the upstage wall is a door to the hall. Downstage of the dressing table on the right is a bentwood rocker. At the head of the bed, on the stage right side, is a small night table with a lamp and an alarm clock on it. It is night-time. The only light is moonlight through the window, stage left. Asleep in bed under the covers is NANCY, an attractive twenty-two year old. There is a knock at the door.

DAVID. *(offstage)* Nancy? ... Nancy, are you awake?
NANCY. *(awakening slowly)* Huh? ... Who is it?

(The door opens and DAVID, a middle-aged man in pajamas, enters and looks around the room, very frightened.)

NANCY. What time is it, Daddy?
DAVID. Sssh! Lower your voice. I heard strange noises. There's somebody out on the terrace. *(He goes to the window and looks out.)*
NANCY. I don't hear anything. You must have had a nightmare.

DAVID. It's no nightmare, I tell you. There's somebody who wants to kill us on the terrace.

NANCY. Daddy, there's nobody on the terrace who wants to kill us.

DAVID. Oh, yeah? How do you know?

NANCY. Because we don't have a terrace.

DAVID. Huh? ... Oh yeah ... uh ... right. We've moved around so much, it's hard to keep track of where we're living.

NANCY. We've only moved twice in twenty-two years.

DAVID. Has it been twenty-two years? Are you that old? Am I that old? We don't look it. So, I ... uh ... guess I should go back to bed.

NANCY. Goodnight, Daddy.

DAVID. Right. Goodnight. *(He kisses her on the cheek, tucks her in, exits the room and closes the door. There's a short pause, then the door opens and he re-enters. He turns on the lamp.)* Nancy, wake up. I've got to talk to you about something. *(She sits up in bed.)* Look, I've been running around like a crazy man scared of something and I didn't know what and now I know what it is. It's that guy.

NANCY. What guy?

DAVID. That guy! The one who wants to marry you tomorrow.

NANCY. You mean Martin?

DAVID. Yeah, that guy.

NANCY. Why do you keep calling him "that guy," like you don't know him? We've been going together for two years. Please call him Martin.

DAVID. Okay, Martin. He's Martin, okay?

NANCY. Okay. Now, what is it you want to say about Martin?

DAVID. *(There's a pause.)* Let's see how I can put this.... You're not marrying him! Get it?! You're not marrying him and that's what I want to say about him. Now, go back to sleep. First thing in the morning we'll figure out the best way to get out of the wedding. Goodnight, sweetheart. *(He kisses her on the forehead, goes quickly out the door and shuts it behind him. There's a beat, and then he comes back in.)* I just thought it over and I'm wrong.... We shouldn't wait until morning to get out of the wedding. We should do it now.... You want to know the logic behind my decision? ... I don't like him..... I mean, I used to like him.... I mean I thought I liked him.... But now there's something about him that scares me. He's going to hurt you, I can feel it.... Do something crazy like get you pregnant on your honeymoon and leave you stranded in the Alps, or force you to change your mind about going to law school and become a punk rock hippie. Or something worse. I don't know what, but I know he's up to no good.... Don't you look at me like *I'm* crazy. I'm your father and if I feel these things there must be truth in them. He's probably got something terrible in his past that he never told us about. Who knows? He might've killed somebody. Two years is nothing to know a person. Come see me after a lifetime, then we'll talk about him.... Look, Nancy, I can't see how you can really be in love with this guy. So he was president of his class and voted most likely to succeed? Big deal. I'm telling you he's got potential good-for-nothing bum written all over him. And don't let his good marks in medical school fool you.

The jails are filled with smart, quack doctors. Sure, his parents are nice people, but we only know them a year and a *half.* Who knows *they* didn't kill somebody? ... Look, I can see I haven't convinced you. So I'm sorry, but I'm going to have to tell you something that's going to hurt your feelings. Nancy, he's not good-looking enough for you. Oh, sure, his face has perfect features. But his ears are very small.... It's a sign of early senility. You can look that up. And long fingers may be great for a surgeon, but they also indicate stinginess. My Uncle Jack had fingers like that. He never bought my cousins a bicycle. You don't want your kids to go without bicycles, do you? ... Please, Nancy, I beg you. Don't marry Melvin.

NANCY. Martin.

DAVID. Melvin, Martin. What the hell's the difference? He still has long ears and small fingers.

NANCY. Small ears and long fingers.

DAVID. Exactly! ... Look, I know you think I'm not making sense but please trust me. Pick up the telephone and tell him very nicely you hate his guts and never want to see him again. If you don't want to hurt him, tell him you have poison ivy all over and you decided to be a nun.... Better yet, send him a telegram. Short and sweet. Goodbye, Charlie. Over and out. Okay, Nancy? ... Alright, I didn't want to do this, but you're forcing me to. I *forbid* you to marry him. I'm your father and under no circumstances will I allow you to marry that man! No way! No chance! No how! It's final! That's it! Because if he ever hurts you, I'll pick him up with both hands and I'll.... *(screaming as he throws powerful punches in the air at an unknown enemy)* ... Bam! Bam! Bam! Bam! Bam! ... Bam!!!

(His flurry of punches is so intense that he almost knocks himself out. He plops down in the bentwood rocker downstage right.)

NANCY. *(Crawls to the edge of the bed and leans on her elbows. Tenderly.)* I'm so glad I talked you into wearing a white tuxedo for the wedding.

DAVID. You don't think it makes me look heavy?

NANCY. You look very dashing, Daddy.

DAVID. You're going to visit us a lot, aren't you? I mean, you're not planning on living too far away, are you?

NANCY. You mean like in the Alps?

DAVID. Well, he says he wants to be a country doctor. I just want to make sure he means this country. *(There is a pause as they smile at each other's joke.)*

DAVID. *(Gets a lump in his throat as a tear comes to his eye.)* He's a nice boy. You did real good.

NANCY. *(Gets up from the bed and sits on his lap.)* I know.

DAVID. Are you nervous about tomorrow?

NANCY. I was, but you calmed me down. Thanks, Daddy. *(She nestles her head on his chest like a little girl. He gently begins rocking back and forth with her in his arms. Lights slowly fade out.)*

BILL AND LAURA

BILL AND LAURA

Lights fade up. The set is an elegantly decorated bedroom in an East Side New York brownstone. There is a double bed with a small mound of coats on it center stage. There is a platformed area upstage of the bed so that one can move freely behind the bed. There are filled book shelves on the upstage center wall. Downstage, on the stage right wall is a makeup table and seat (no back). Just upstage of the makeup table is a door to a hallway. Downstage left is a sitting area consisting of a love seat, an end chair and a coffee table. In the center of the stage left wall is a door to the bathroom. There is a large plant in the upstage left corner and a chair and floor lamp in the upstage right corner. There are appropriately tasteful paintings on the walls. GRACE, an elegantly dressed older woman, enters, followed by a younger couple, HANK and LAURA.

HANK. ...And then the first guy says to him, "Well, what did you expect to happen, pal. We're in a bathroom." *(HANK and GRACE burst out laughing. LAURA laughs politely.)*

GRACE. Oh, Hank, you are so witty. *(to LAURA)* Isn't that the wittiest joke you've ever heard?

LAURA. *(trying to sound convincing)* Very witty. He's a ... uh ... real wit.

GRACE. Excuse me, dear, is it Joan or Jeanette?

LAURA. Laura.

13

GRACE. Where did I get Joan or Jeanette?...

HANK. Because Joan or Jeanette was my date for your last party. *(Again, GRACE and HANK laugh convulsively. LAURA forces another laugh. HANK continues to LAURA.)* I'll go get us some champagne, doll, and then I'm going to tell you the one I heard about the bowlegged hooker and the hunchback who was a sissy. *(He laughs and pinches GRACE who laughs too. Then, HANK exits back into the hall. LAURA and GRACE are now alone in the room. LAURA takes off her coat and puts it on the bed. They stand at the foot of the bed.)*

GRACE. Hank tells me that you're recently divorced.

LAURA. Separated.

GRACE. Well, speaking candidly, I have friends who would love to be in your shoes. Hank is considered the biggest catch in our runners' club.

LAURA. Right. I'm a lucky woman.... Uh ... do you have any aspirin?

GRACE. Surely, follow me. *(LAURA follows GRACE into the bathroom. As they enter the bathroom, NORM [GRACE'S husband] enters the room with another couple, BILL [a middle-aged man] and TERRI [a buxom woman in her early twenties]).*

NORM. *(to BILL)* I'm proud to be handling your account, Bill. *(to TERRI as he takes her coat)* And what's your name?

BILL. Oh ... uh ... Norm, this is Terri....

NORM. Pleased to meet you.

TERRI. Do you have any Armond Anteater?

NORM. Huh?

TERRI. They're a new wave group. Do you have Phil and the Flea Bites? ... Sick Sidney and his Pups? ... The Dead Rabbits? ... Can I go check your records?

NORM. Be my guest. *(She exits into hall. NORM eyes her lecherously as she goes.)* Delightful. You got the right idea, Bill. When I split with my first wife, I only dated women my own age. They were well-read and they were annoying.

(The doorbell rings.)

NORM. Whoops. Gotta go play host. *(NORM exits into hall. BILL walks toward stage right side of the bed with his coat. As he reaches the bed, the bathroom door opens and GRACE and LAURA reenter the room. LAURA's and BILL's eyes meet. GRACE goes to shake BILL's hand.)*

GRACE. I'm so glad you could come to our party. Excuse me. I have to go see how my mousse is settling. *(GRACE rushes out of the room. There is a long pause as LAURA and BILL look at each other. LAURA is on the stage left side of the bed.)*

BILL. What are you doing here?

LAURA. Date. What are you doing here?

BILL. Date.

LAURA. I got here first. You leave.

BILL. I'm here on business. You leave.

LAURA. I'm staying.

BILL. So am I.

LAURA. Up your nose.

BILL. Out your ear.

GRACE. *(Sticks her head into the room.)* My mousse settled perfectly. Come in the dining room. We're serving the croudite. *(She goes back out.)*

BILL. You don't want to leave. Fine. Just do me a favor.

Don't talk to me for the rest of the evening. Don't even look at me.

LAURA. Look at you? It's a dinner party. Why would I want to ruin my appetite?

BILL. That's it! We don't wait for the divorce. We go to Reno. I want it now!

LAURA. You got it. Let's eat. *(They walk towards the door. They bump shoulders as they try to go through the doorway at the same time.)*

BILL. Alright, look, this is going to be a very difficult evening. Let's try to be civil to each other, at least until the meal is over. Okay?

LAURA. Fine.

BILL. Good.

LAURA. Great.

BILL. You still have to get the last word.

LAURA. Right. *(They go out the door. The lights fade out. In the blackout we hear the sounds of a party coming to life: music, chatter, etc. The lights fade up on the same room. There is now a mountain of coats on the bed. LAURA enters the room followed by BILL.)* I'm leaving! Where's my coat?

BILL. I'm leaving first!

LAURA. *(Goes to the stage right side of the bed. He goes to the stage left side and they start sifting through the large pile of coats to find theirs.)* How dare you humiliate me in front of all those people by looking at my date with such contempt?

BILL. I don't even know who your date is, Miss. Who is it, the short, fat, bald guy with the lisp? I happen to like him for you.

LAURA. You know perfectly well who my date is. The

tall, handsome, free-spirited gentleman with the wide shoulders.

BILL. Oh, that clown. Where did you meet him? At a Halloween party for obnoxious people?

LAURA. Jealous, aren't you?

BILL. Of what? His subtle sense of humor? That was a very classy joke he was telling about the Sumo wrestler with the hemorrhoids. So, how long have you been dating your new Prince Charming? Let me guess. Ever since he showed you his collection of whoopie cushions.

LAURA. I'm sorry you have such a low opinion of my date because I'm very impressed with yours. Where did you meet *her?* Across the counter at McDonald's? I know, it was the uniform that attracted you. You should marry her because you've got so much to share. You can watch Scooby Do together and explain the plots to her. *(They each find their coats. She goes to the door.)*

BILL. *(Stops her.)* Are you sleeping with Mr. Gong Show winner?

LAURA. Why? Are you sleeping with Miss Bowling Alley Beauty Contest loser?

BILL. *(Grabs her mink from her.)* Give me that coat. That's a fifteen thousand dollar investment.)

LAURA. *(Grabs his coat from him.)* And I bought this to keep you warm.

BILL. I don't want you bringing that laughing lame brain around my kids.

GRACE. *(The hostess sticks her head in the room. Cheerfully.)* The vichyssoise is being served.

LAURA. *(ignoring her)* Don't you dare tell me how to live my life. I'll bring around whoever I want.

BILL. That's it! You're not getting the house.

LAURA. That's it! I'm getting the house *and* the sailboat.

GRACE. Do you two know each other?

BILL. *(to GRACE)* Excuse me, we're talking. *(He ushers her out of the door and closes it.)* I'm going to demand half the furniture, the dishes, the linens, and the towels. His and hers!

LAURA. And I'm going after your desk, your books and your own personal computer.

BILL. Oh, yeah? Well, from now on I'm keeping little Tommy with me.

LAURA. Over my dead body will you get the cat!

BILL. I've gone out of my way to be fair with the settlement. But, now I'm going to see that you end up with nothing but the twelve pairs of designer jeans that you came into the marriage with.

LAURA. And by the time my lawyer and I get through with you, you'll end up with what you came into the marriage with — a bunch of socks and underwear that match. Oh, and Hank, my date, will look good in that suit you're wearing after they tear it off you in the court-room.

BILL. I'd like to grab him by the throat, bang his head against the wall and choke him until his eyes pop out!

LAURA. Who, my date?

BILL. No, your lawyer.

LAURA. Don't you dare insult my lawyer. He's the only man I ever trusted.

(The door opens and GRACE sticks her head in.)

GRACE. Excuse me, I don't know if you're aware, but this is a sit-down dinner.

LAURA. Who cares? This is a divorce. *(She closes the door on her. To BILL)* My lawyer is the only man who ever cared about what's best for me.

BILL. Your lawyer is a sneak, a snake and a husband-hater.

LAURA. My lawyer is a saint next to the Neanderthal that represents you.

BILL. You're just threatened because I hired a woman. *(He turns and walks smugly and sits in the upstage left end chair.)*

LAURA. Au contraire. I happen to admire all her qualities, especially the hair on her hands. *(She sits on the love seat.)*

BILL. Do you know she was so outraged by your ingratitude toward me she begged to take my case. And I had to force her to take a fee.

LAURA. Well, I hope you and your philanthropic vampire will be very happy together. I am so thrilled to be away from you. You held me back all these years. Now, I'm free. I can soar like an eagle.

BILL. I've seen your date. If you're soaring like an eagle, your co-pilot's a limp turkey.

LAURA. *(Rises, goes to the makeup table and leans against it.)* For your information, Hank is just one of many many men I'm dating. And I'm getting something from each of them that I never got from you. Jeff is so interested in every word I have to say that he never speaks. That's love. From Edgar, I get the freedom to be mopey and grumpy all the time I'm with him because he says my mopey and grumpy is better than other women's happy and loving. From Maurice, I get the sensitivity of a man who cares for me so much that it's enough for him just to color my hair and shop for fabrics with me.

BILL. *(Rises and crosses to LAURA and sits on the seat.)* Oh, yeah? I suppose you think Terri is the only girl I'm seeing. You think I'm just dating college kids? I'm out with a different girl every night, baby. And every one of them is great. From Ginger, I get all the intellectual stimulation I need. She's a psychiatrist in a woman's prison. We have great conversations about feminine violence. From Joanne, I get the security of someone who loves me so much she'd throw herself in front of a truck to save my life. And she has. Right on Eighth Avenue and 43rd Street. At this moment, she's in Roosevelt Hospital recovering from four broken ribs. Top that for devotion, baby.

LAURA. You call that devotion? I call that sick in the head. You obviously have no talent whatsoever for being single. And I'm doing all the things that I couldn't do because I was too stifled when I was married to you.

BILL. *(He rises and they confront each other nose to nose.)* Oh yeah? Like what?

LAURA. Aerobics.

BILL. I'm playing raquetball.

LAURA. I'm taking a class on weaving in straw.

BILL. I'm learning to cook nouvelle American cuisine.

LAURA. I'm the same weight I was in college.

BILL. My pulse rate is down.

LAURA. I rewallpapered the guest room.

BILL. I may buy a condominium.

LAURA. It sounds like your life is dog waste!

BILL. Your life is elephant waste.

LAURA. I never hit you when we were married, but it would be my pleasure to deck you now.

BILL. Go ahead and hit me. Blanche, my lawyer, would love it.

LAURA. Ooo, I would just love to.... *(She looks around the room.)*

BILL. You want to throw something at me, don't you? Poor thing. You're in someone else's apartment so you can't.

LAURA. *(She rushes to the stage right side of the bed. He goes to the stage left side. She finds her pocketbook and opens it.)* I can't, huh? How about my lipstick? *(She throws it at him.)*

BILL. *(He ducks.)* Wait a minute. This is a dinner party. *(He runs upstage around the head of the bed.)*

LAURA. How about my Vitamin C? *(She throws a handful of vitamins. He ducks.)*

GRACE. *(Opens the door.)* How about my Salmon En Crote?

LAURA. *(to GRACE)* How about my Kleenex? *(She throws them at GRACE. GRACE quickly leaves and closes the door. BILL locks it. LAURA returns to BILL)* How about my credit cards?! *(She throws her credit cards at him.)*

BILL. Great! I've been trying to get my hands on these! *(He starts picking them up.)*

LAURA. Give me those!

BILL. Give me those pearls! *(He pulls her pearls over her head.)*

LAURA. Give me that watch. *(She pulls his watch off and*

*goes to the stage right side of the bed. He goes to the stage left side
and they begin throwing coats off the bed as they yell at each other.)*
I hate you!

BILL. I hate you!

LAURA. I hate you first!

BILL. I hate you most!

LAURA. I hate you best! ...

BILL. I love being separated from you!

LAURA. I don't need you!

BILL. I don't need you! I never needed you!

LAURA. I don't want to need you!

BILL. I can make it without you!

LAURA. So can I!

BILL. I need you! I need you so much! *(Tears come to
his eyes.)*

LAURA. I miss you, Billy. *(Tears come to her eyes.)*

BILL. I can't make it without you.

LAURA. I hate this separation.

BILL. This is a miserable separation. *(They kiss and start
pulling the covers off the bed. The coats are now on the floor.)*

LAURA. *(as they kiss romantically)* I think we're holding
up dinner.

BILL. *(continuing to kiss her)* Let 'em eat Quiche. *(They
continue to kiss and disappear under the covers. Lights fade
out.)*

ALAN, BETTY AND RIVA

ALAN, BETTY AND RIVA

Scene One

The lights come up on a small old-fashioned hotel room. It's night time. The room was at one time fashionable but is now frayed around the edges. A double bed is against the center of the stage left wall. There is a bottle of champagne in an ice bucket and a radio on the upstage night table and a telephone on the night table on the other side of the bed. A small mechanical alarm clock sits next to the phone. A fireplace with a mirror above it is in the stage right wall. Upstage center are French door-type windows leading to a small balcony with a wrought iron railing and posts supporting the balcony above. The windows are about three feet from the floor. Upstage left is a door leading to the bathroom. Upstage right is the door to the room. ALAN lights a cigarette and paces nervously, looking at his watch. There is a knock at the door.

ALAN. Betty?

BETTY. *(offstage)* Yes, Alan.

ALAN. One second. *(He quickly puts out the cigarette, turns the lights down low, straightens his hair in the front of the mirror, puts soft music on the radio, gives himself a blast of breath spray, and opens the door.)* Hi.

25

BETTY. Hello, Alan. *(She's wearing a coat and a white nurse's hat.)*

ALAN. Come on in.

BETTY. Alan, I don't know if I should. *(He takes her by the hand, closes the door and leads her to the center of the room.)*

ALAN. Sure you should.

BETTY. Alan. It doesn't seem right.

ALAN. You know it's right. Otherwise you wouldn't be here in this hotel room with me. *(He starts kissing her seductively on the neck.)*

BETTY. Oh, Alan, I love you so much. I would do anything for you. *(They kiss passionately.)*

(They hear a door open. They look at each other. The bathroom door opens and RIVA comes out, dressed in a sexy slip and negligee, with a towel over her shoulder, carrying a thermos. RIVA walks over to them in the center of the room so that ALAN is standing between BETTY and RIVA.)

ALAN. Uh ... Riva, this is Betty .... Uh ... Betty, Riva.

RIVA. How do you do? This is hysterical. You are not going to believe this. I have the exact same shoes, only with a more open back and a higher heel.

BETTY. Uh ... really? *(Starts to faint. ALAN catches her.)*

RIVA. *(to ALAN)* Is this her first time in a triple?

ALAN. Yeah.

RIVA. I see. Well, take your time. Pressure never works. *(Goes to the end table, picks up the phone, dials, puts the phone to her ear, and starts winding up the alarm clock.)*

ALAN. *(to BETTY)* Let me take your coat. *(He helps her remove the coat. She's wearing a nurse's uniform underneath it.*

He takes the coat, quickly throws it into the closet and goes back to BETTY.)

RIVA. *(into phone as she sits seductively on the edge of the bed)* Hello, Mr. Henry, this is Riva Gauche Champignon. The Sex Therapist. *(BETTY begins to faint again.)*

ALAN. *(Catches her.)* Would you like to dance?

RIVA. *(into phone)* I'm calling because I have a conflict tonight at eight. *(ALAN dances BETTY over towards the bed.)*

BETTY. Let's have a cigarette. *(She breaks free from ALAN and backs away.)*

ALAN. *(He pursues.)* You don't smoke.

BETTY. I don't? *(As BETTY continues to evade ALAN, RIVA sticks her leg out and stops her. BETTY freezes, frightened. To ALAN.)* Let's talk. *(BETTY crawls across the bed to get away from RIVA and then sits on the far corner of the bed.)*

ALAN. *(Walks around the bed after her.)* Betty, you don't want to talk.

BETTY. Alan, if we don't talk, I'm leaving.

ALAN. *(He crawls on the bed and sits next to BETTY. RIVA goes to the back corner of bed. She ends up on the other side of ALAN.)* Okay, okay.... Did you enjoy your lunch today?

BETTY. Yes.

RIVA. *(into phone)* I have a cocktail party with an IBM group at 5:30 and a luau at seven.

ALAN. Your fillet of sole wasn't dry?

BETTY. No, it wasn't dry.

RIVA. *(into phone)* I'm wondering if you and your lovely wife would come at 8:30 in case I run over?

ALAN. How was the dessert? Did you like your berries?

BETTY. Yes, they were good berries.

RIVA. *(into phone)* I will call Mr. and Mrs. Smith and tell them 8:30 is fine with you. *(RIVA puts her hand on ALAN's thigh.)*

ALAN. *(He puts BETTY's hand on his other thigh.)* Boy, I feel so relaxed. *(He puts one arm around BETTY's shoulder and the other one around RIVA.)*

RIVA. *(Takes this as a cue and snuggles up to him with the phone still to her ear. Into phone.)* You would rather do it? *(BETTY turns her head slowly. Her eyes meet RIVA's. RIVA smiles and winks at her. BETTY gets up and moves to foot of bed.)*

ALAN. *(whispering to RIVA)* This is harder than I thought.

RIVA. *(wispering to ALAN)* Hang in there. *(into phone)* Fine, you call them.

ALAN. *(whispering to RIVA)* I'm tryling to do this in a sensitive way.

RIVA. *(whispering to ALAN)* You're a class guy. *(into phone)* But please call me back and confirm. My whole reputation is based on my running like clockwork.

ALAN. *(whispering to RIVA)* Why is it taking so long?

RIVA. *(whispering to ALAN)* She ain't hot yet. *(into phone)* I wouldn't ever want to be badmouthed for over-lapping. Bye.

ALAN. I'd better go relax her.

RIVA. If you need any help, let me know.

ALAN. Uh ... no ... uh ... not yet. *(He gets up and goes over to BETTY at the foot of the bed. To BETTY.)* What is it, honey?

BETTY. You think she's prettier than me!

ALAN. *(Kneels in front of BETTY and holds her in an effort to console her and get her back to the head of the bed. Whispering.)* Are you kidding? I don't find her attractive at all. She's just here to make it better for us. *(They both look over at RIVA. She nods in agreement.)*

BETTY. If I do this, you won't love me anymore. *(RIVA has taken out her bills, checkbook, pen and appointment book and is completely involved in settling her personal accounts.)*

ALAN. *(Leads BETTY back to the head of the bed and begins to uncork the champagne.)* Betty, I told you. I'm going to love you more. Much, much, much more. I already do just from your coming here. Don't you see that your accepting the part of me that wants to do this gives me the room to love you more? Come on, let me give you some champagne. *(He pours her a glass of champagne and gives it to her. RIVA is drinking soup from a thermos.)*

ALAN. *(Toasts.)* Here's to love.

BETTY. And marriage.

RIVA. And the most important thing of all — good health. *(They clink glasses, RIVA using the plastic cup from her thermos.)*

ALAN. *(Puts his hand under BETTY's glass and tips it up.)* Go ahead, drink up.

BETTY. *(staring at RIVA who's now taking her stockings off)* Alan, I'm not the type.

ALAN. Everybody's the type if you're loving. Didn't you say this was your fantasy too?

BETTY. No, Alan, you said it was your fantasy and it was important to you to make it my fantasy, so I did. But this is different. This is dirty.

ALAN. That's what's good about it. Fantasies have to be

dirty or they're not fantasies. They're just sordid reality. Come on, we're here. Let's give it our best shot.

BETTY. She's not young enough. And that's not her own hair color.

ALAN. You close your eyes, you make her into whatever you want.

RIVA. *(Begins taking off ALAN's shoes.)* Yeah!

ALAN. What have you got to lose? I paid her already. *(He takes BETTY's hand and puts it back on his leg.)*

BETTY. What if somebody finds out?

ALAN. How's anybody going to find out? She's not going to tell anyone. Are you?

RIVA. *(now taking off ALAN's socks)* Nooooo!

ALAN. Come on. Next time you can pick whoever you want.

BETTY. *(Takes her hand off his leg.)* Next time? You never said anything about a next time. I don't like this at all. *(She tries to crawl off the bed.)*

ALAN. *(Catches her at the edge.)* Shh. Do you want to hurt her feelings? *(RIVA has followed him and starts to undress him, first his shirt and tie.)*

BETTY. If this is so loving, why haven't you ever done this with Charlene?

ALAN. Shhhh! I don't want her to know our business.

BETTY. Why have you never done this with your wife, Dr. Flerm?

RIVA. *(to ALAN)* Yeah.

ALAN. *(to both girls)* I never did this with Charlene because I never had the need to keep it exciting with Charlene. Because it never was exciting with Charlene. But with you it was exciting right from the beginning. But four years have passed since we first fell in love. And with you I want to keep it new and exciting. Charlene doesn't deserve this. I don't love her. I love you.

BETTY. Then how come you haven't left her, Alan?

RIVA. *(to ALAN)* Yeah.

ALAN. *(As he answers, RIVA is rubbing his chest. He's getting excited.)* I haven't left her because it's never been the right time. And this is my way of making it the right time, by making it so exciting with you that I have to leave her. See, I've arranged all this to finally get me to make the decision I've wanted to make for four years but couldn't do because of my morality, integrity, and the fear of what the scandal would do to my chiropodist practice. *(RIVA takes BETTY's hand and puts it on ALAN's chest.)*

BETTY. *(rubbing ALAN's chest)* Oh, Alan, do you mean that?

ALAN. *(panting)* I really hope so. *(RIVA takes ALAN's pants off.)*

BETTY. Oh, Alan, you're everything I live for. *(They embrace.)*

ALAN. *(almost out of his mind)* Oh, this is the most exciting thing that's ever happened to me. *(RIVA unbuttons one button of BETTY's nursing uniform.)* Say it's exciting for you too.

BETTY. *(looking at RIVA's hand)* Must I?

ALAN. Please, it's important to me. Say it, Betty.

BETTY. Oh, Alan, it's exciting for me, too.

ALAN. *(to RIVA)* Say it's exciting for you too.

RIVA. *(blasé)* It's exciting for me too.

ALAN. *(pleadingly)* Can you say it like you mean it? "Alan, it's exciting for me too."

RIVA. *(excited)* Alan, it's exciting for me too.

ALAN. *(Puts his head back and closes hie eyes.)* Good. Touch me. I feel alive. *(He motions to them to repeat. BETTY closes her eyes.)*

BOTH GIRLS. Touch me. I feel alive ... Touch me. I feel alive...

(Lights slowly fade out.)

Scene Two

The lights fade up. It is the same room a short time later. BETTY's clothes are strewn on the floor. The three of them are under the sheets, ALAN in the middle. BETTY sticks her head out.

BETTY. *(with great agony)* I can't believe you made me do it, Alan. How can I look at myself in the mirror again. I have never felt so low in my life.

RIVA. *(Sticks her head out. To BETTY.)* Can you help me find my other stocking, honey? *(ALAN sticks his head out, takes the stocking from around his neck, and sheepishly hands it to RIVA, who begins putting it on.)*

BETTY. I hated every minute of it. Even the parts I enjoyed.

ALAN. I didn't even *enjoy* the parts I enjoyed. I thought it would be twice as much fun, but it was twice as much work and I think I pulled something in my groin.

BETTY. I'll tell you who did enjoy it. She did. *(She lunges over ALAN, grabs RIVA by the hair with both hands and begins yanking RIVA's head back and forth. RIVA remains blasé.)* I hate her! I hate her! She ruined our love!

ALAN. I know just how you feel. She could have stopped it at any time. She's the pro here. She used us. She's a devious, kinky, perverted, nympho bisexual.

BETTY. *(letting go of RIVA's hair)* Oh my God, what does that make me?! Why did you *make* me do this disgusting thing, Alan? Why? *(RIVA starts putting nail polish on the runs in her stockings.)*

ALAN. I made you do this disgusting thing to make us so new and exciting it would force me to ask Charlene for a divorce.

BETTY. So when are you going to ask Charlene for the divorce?

ALAN. Huh?

BETTY. I want an answer right now, Alan.

ALAN. Look, Betty. I love you because you're so ... pliable and I hate Charlene because she's so ... stagnant. If I can make her pliable enough to leave me without upsetting the kids, and if you can make yourself stagnant enough to hang in there until I can find a way for you to move in with me without upsetting my chiropodist practice in New Rochelle, *that's* when I'll ask her.

RIVA. Look at all the runs in my stockings.

BETTY. I hate you, Alan! I hate you! You're never going to leave Charlene. I have nothing to live for!

(The alarm clock goes off.)

RIVA. *(Shuts it off.)* Time's up. You're a lovely couple and I've enjoyed working with you. But... *(BETTY gets up, as if in a trance, goes over to the French doors and opens them.)* ...I must ask you to vacate my room now because I need time to pull myself together between stimulations.

BETTY. I'm going to throw myself out the window! *(She steps up onto the ledge and climbs over the railing, holding on to the pole.)*

ALAN. No! Are you crazy? Get off there! *(ALAN and*

RIVA go to the window.)

RIVA. Get off there. I have customers coming. You'll fall right on top of them.

BETTY. I'm going to jump!

ALAN. *(frantically)* Betty, I beg you, don't jump!

BETTY. I'm jumping!!

RIVA. This is annoying.

ALAN. Betty, please, you have so much to live for. Doesn't she?

RIVA. Absolutely. She's a real charmer.

BETTY. To hell with New Rochelle! To hell with your practice!!

RIVA. Look, why don't you two go do this over a beer someplace? The Dworfmans will be here any minute.

BETTY. You made me a bisexual!

ALAN. The Dworfmans? Petey and Jane Dworfman?

RIVA. I think so.

BETTY. I came here a something and now I'm a nothing.

ALAN. *(aghast)* They're friends of Charlene. We've got to get out of here. Betty, please get off the ledge!

(A buzzer rings. RIVA goes to the intercom box on the stage right wall next to the hall door and puts earphone up to her ear.)

BETTY. This is what I get for loving too much.

RIVA. *(into the intercom)* Yeah? ...

ALAN. Betty, I love you too much too.

BETTY. But you don't love me too much to leave Charlene, so I'm jumping.

RIVA. *(to ALAN)* Dammit, it's the Dworfmans. *(She looks*

at herself in the mirror on the wall next to the intercom) **And look at how I look.** *(into the intercom)* **Tell them they'll have to wait a minute.** *(She hangs up the intercom and crosses to the bathroom)*

ALAN. Betty, please, the Dworfmans are downstairs. They'll hear you!

BETTY. Screw the Dworfmans! You're not leaving Charlene. I degrade myself and this is the thanks I get.

ALAN.   Where are my thanks? *(to RIVA, who's brushing her teeth in the bathroom)* Didn't I degrade myself?

RIVA. Absolutely. Look, Miss, Dr. Flerm here signed you up for six more treatments. Come off the ledge and we'll spend the whole next time talking about how you degraded yourselves, okay?

BETTY. *(outraged, to ALAN)* You signed me up for six of these humiliating treatments without telling me?

ALAN. *(frantically)* It was half off for six!

BETTY. Alan, unless you tell Charlene you're leaving her, I'm going spread eagle and if I take the Dworfmans with me, so be it.

ALAN. Betty, please listen to reason.

BETTY. I'm through listening to your reason. I want a promise!

ALAN. Betty....

BETTY. Promise!

ALAN. Betty....

RIVA. *(putting on lip gloss)* Promise her, already! You're giving me a headache!

ALAN. Alright, I promise! Now come down off there!

BETTY. On your children's heads!

ALAN. Betty, please....

BETTY. On your children's heads! *(ALAN hesitates.)*

RIVA. *(Comes out of the bathroom, curling her eyebrows.)* Look, I've gone out of my way to be courteous, but if she doesn't get off the ledge, I'm going to have to call the police. This is not good for my therapy business.

BETTY. Your children's heads, Alan!

ALAN. Alright! On my children's heads.

BETTY. *(Climbs over the railing and comes back into the room.)* Oh, Alan, I love you. Can you ever forgive me? *(They embrace.)*

ALAN. I forgive you. Can you forgive me?

BETTY. Alan, you know I forgive you. *(They kiss like two little mice. RIVA begins straightening the bed and picking up all of their loose clothing.)*

ALAN. Let's forgive Riva too.

BETTY. I forgive you.

ALAN. I forgive you.

RIVA. *(Hands them their clothes in a lump.)* Thanks, your a gracious couple. *(She begins ushering them to the door.)* You can dress in the back stairway and walk down to the parking lot. No one will see you.

BETTY. We forgive you, Riva.

ALAN. We forgive you.

RIVA. *(as she opens the door)* Right. I forgive you too. *(They go out the door.)*

ALAN. *(Turns back to RIVA.)* Was it really exciting for you?

RIVA. Right. Multiple orgasms. *(He exits. RIVA closes the*

door behind him. Half aloud to herself.) What a way to make a living. *(She picks up the intercom and talks into it.)* Send up the Dworfmans, Manny.

(Lights fade out.)

NICK AND WENDY

NICK AND WENDY

Scene One

The lights fade up. The set is a large first-class Southern California hotel room. The furnishing is bright and very tasteful. The door to the room is downstage left. Upstage left there is a sitting area consisting of a couch, two end chairs and cocktail table. There are end tables with lamps on each side of the couch which is against the wall. At the stage left side of the upstage wall are sliding glass doors that lead to a first floor private patio. There is a patio table and chairs and there is a high wooden, ivy-covered fence enclosing the patio. Against the stage right side of the upstage wall is a long, low dresser with a lamp on it. On the wall above the dresser is a large understated abstract painting. At the upstage end of the stage right wall is a door to the bathroom. Downstage of the bathroom, against the stage right wall, are two single beds with a night table and lamp between them. There are suitcase stands at the foot of each bed. The door is opened with a key and a bellman enters carrying two small suitcases and a cosmetic case. He's followed by NICK and WENDY.

BELLMAN. Where would you like your bags?
NICK. Put this one over here.... No, put it over there. No, in the closet. No, put the little one in the bathroom.

(He puts one of the suitcases on the stand at the foot of the downstage bed.)

WENDY. You can put mine anywhere, anywhere at all. I'm just so happy to be here. I don't care about anything

BELLMAN. Are you here for the real estate convention or the antique furniture fair? *(He takes the cosmetic case and the other suitcase into the bathroom/dressing room. NICK and WENDY stand downstage center.)*

NICK. Uh ... we're just ... uh ... tourists.

WENDY. We're here for the self-encounter weekend seminar.

BELLMAN. *(Comes out of the bathroom.)* Oh, yeah, they're here every month. Funny, you don't look like the type. He does, but you don't.

NICK. What does that mean?

BELLMAN. *(Stands between NICK and WENDY.)* Usually the women who come for that wear pant suits and no jewelry and they seem miserable.

WENDY. Thank you for the compliment. You see, my days of being miserable are over. *(She smiles and gives NICK a look. She walks around the room talking animatedly.)* This is going to be the beginning of a new life, a new me, a new inner journey to the unknown. A new....

NICK. *(Quickly takes the key from the BELLMAN and gives him a tip.)* Here, thank you. *(He takes him by the arm and leads him out the door.)*

WENDY. *(Throws open the drapes.)* Oh, I never thought a second smog alert could be so beautiful. But I guess when you're willing to find out who you really are, everything takes on a new beauty. Don't you think so, Nick?

NICK. Do you realize what a stupid moron you just made of yourself?

WENDY. Nick, a week ago what you just said would have destroyed me. But I'm changing. You just can't hurt me anymore with your name calling, you big jerk.

NICK. I'm a jerk? Who's forty years old and doesn't know who she really is? Me? From day one, I've known who I am.

WENDY. Well, I guess that's what makes people different. I don't know who I am and you've always known you're a big jerk.

NICK. I'm leaving.

WENDY. Put that suitcase down.

NICK. *(Heads for the door with one of the suitcases.)* I should have never let you talk me into this. You want to stay? Stay! I'm getting the hell out of here.

WENDY. If you leave, the marriage is over. Because then there's no hope, and I can't live with that.

NICK. *(Turns to her.)* Don't you threaten me with no hope!

WENDY. Don't you threaten me with leaving! You made a commitment, you have to keep it. *(She holds up a piece of paper she's been carrying.)* That's what the brochure says. The first step to making your life work is keeping commitments. Are you going to stay and face your worst fears like a powerful man, or are you going to run away from them like a sniveling sissy?

NICK. *(Slams the door.)* How dare you ask an ex-Marine that question? You're a bigger sissy than I'll ever be! *(He pushes past WENDY and heads for the phone on the night table between the beds. He picks it up and begins dialing.)* I need a drink.

WENDY. Oh, no. You know the ground rules. *(She picks*

up the brochure and reads.) "No alcohol, no tobacco, no pain killers, no coffee, no candy, no gum, and no food except for the one prescribed meal."

NICK. *(He slams the phone down.)* You're going to keep all those rules that were made up by some skinny jerk on top of a mountain in Tibet who never tasted a candy bar in his life?

WENDY. Only a sub-idiot would call a Zen master a jerk.

NICK. Oh, yeah? And what about the bathroom break? You're going to go five hours without going to the bathroom?

WENDY. That's right.

NICK. Not with your bladder, baby.

WENDY. Nick, I signed an agreement. And I'm going to keep it even if I wet my pants in front of two hundred and fifty people. That's how much integrity I have. How much integrity do you have, Mr. ex-Marine, tough guy?

NICK. Alright. I'll keep the stupid agreements. I went through boot camp. I can go through this crap. *(He sits in the downstage chair.)*

WENDY. Good. Now at least we can begin to deal with all our problems.

NICK. What do you mean our problems? Your problems. I don't have any problems. I'm thrilled with my life.

WENDY. You're thrilled with your life?

NICK. That's right.

WENDY. You don't have any problems?

NICK. Not one.

WENDY. *(Approaches his chair slowly like a prosecuting attorney.)* What about your business? The children? My going back to work? How do you feel about my brother? That you don't trust any of your friends. That you didn't cry at your father's funeral. That you're afraid of black cats. That the only feeling you ever show is what a bully you are. That Dr. Goldman said unless you cry, you are prime heart attack material. That we haven't had sex in almost three weeks.

NICK. You're not going to mention any of those things, are you?

WENDY. *(sitting on the coffee table next to him)* Nick, the whole thing about this weekend is being real. I have to get up in front of two hundred and fifty people and let every rotten thing about you hang out.

NICK. Look, if you feel you have to talk about me, do it, but don't mention my name.

WENDY. *(sitting across from him)* Nick, I'm sorry, but I have to mention your name. All these years we've been playing a game called, "Let's not tell Nick how full of shit he is." I can't play anymore games if I want to reach the full potential, not only of the self I am in Sherman Oaks but.... *(reading from the brochure)* "Of the total self I am in the cosmos." Telling the truth about your wretched negativity is the key to my growth.

NICK. Nobody has to know I'm the husband your're accusing. Mention my name if you have to, but don't point to me.

WENDY. Nick, I have to mention your name and point to you. It's time for you to find out that crime does not pay. Let's go to the seminar. *(She gets up, walks to the door and opens it.)* I'm waiting, Nick. *(NICK slowly turns and walks to the door, as if he were on his way to the electric chair.)* Big Jerk. *(She exits after him and closes the door behind her.)*

(Lights fade out.)

Scene Two

The lights fade up. It is the same room, four hours later. The door opens. WENDY enters first, followed by NICK. WENDY looks like she is in shock. NICK is grinning smugly. He closes the door behind him, as she lies down on the downstage bed. There is a long pause. Then he slowly starts pacing around the room triumphantly.

NICK. What a great experience this is. What was I so afraid of? I mean, when you got up there in front of all those people and said those things and they told you how full of shit you are, it was like an enormous burden off my back. I mean, I went in that room scared because deep down inside I thought I was the bad guy. That's a laugh. Even when I was a kid and I was hitting my sisters with bricks, I wasn't such a bad guy. I was only doing it to be noticed. It was as if I was saying, "Hey, look at me. I need love too." You want me to be a bully so you can be a victim. It's like you keep putting your face underneath my foot. I keep trying to take it away, and you keep holding it there. I'm not sure why, but my gut tells me it's got something to do with your needing the excitement. That's just one little insight I got there. Boy, I can really feel myself transforming from this experience. I'm pulling the covers off you, you paranoid, martyr, bitch, nag. Now don't take that as a judgement. It's not your fault. You picked it up from your mother and she picked it up from

46

her mother. Probably your whole family tree, all the way back to the beginning of evolution, is like that. The first turtle who crawled out of the sea who you're related to had to be a whiner, a complainer, and a ball breaker. But I want you to be clear on this. I'm not talking about you all the time. There are moments when you seem perfect. I'm talking about the other ninety percent of the time. When you're not only bad, you're evil. That's what those two hundred and fifty people were reacting to when they booed you. Not the perfect part; the bad, evil, shit part. And that's what you're going to have to change, baby, or it's the garbage dump for you.

WENDY. *(Gets up from the bed.)* Excuse me, I have to go to the bathroom.

NICK. That's what the break is for. *(She goes in the bathroom and closes the door. NICK talks loudly enough for her to hear him through the door.)* Personally, I feel so good that I'm going to wait until the next break just to prove that my body doesn't control me, I control my body. I know they really hurt you in there and you're feeling scared. Don't worry, I'm not going to leave you at your age. You're just going to have to change. I've had it up to here with your neuroses, which are mainly that you're boring, you're a complainer and you're a stupid moron. And don't you ever call me a jerk again. Oh, what a relief to know that I'm not guilty when I hate you, because you created my hate by acting detestable. That's another insight I got in there. *(He looks at his watch.)* Okay. Let's go back in there. I've got to warn you. I'm telling all. My fourteen-year-old son smokes dope and you did it with your permissive attitude. And you're the one who's responsible for my business going in the toilet last year by making me hire your stupid brother who's a total incompetent at $400 a week plus expenses. And I've got to tell them my sex life stinks because you're uptight all the time. I'm going to tell it all, Wendy.

WENDY. *(Comes out of the bathroom.)* You do, and I'll never speak to you again, Nickie.

NICK. What have you got in your mouth? Give it to me.... *(She spits it in his hand.)* Cheese! Wait till I tell them you ate cheese on the break. You little sneak! *(She storms out. He stops and thinks for a moment.)* This place is going to be the making of me. What a jerk I was to put off my openness. *(He goes out.)*

(Lights fade out.)

Scene Three

Lights fade up on the same room. Redish sunlight is coming in through the sliding glass doors, indicating dusk. The door opens and they enter. He's holding his neck and walking stiffly. She's laughing.

WENDY. *(laughing)* That was the most hilarious time I've ever had. You made such a total ass of yourself.

NICK. Will you shut up? I think I pulled something in my neck from tension. Get the house doctor. *(He lies down on the upstage bed.)*

WENDY. Showing them my cheese cube. *(She sits on the bed next to him. Continuing to laugh.)* Those people out there were perceptive enough to see through your facade and call all your insights pure caca. They proved what I suspected about you from day one. You are a blow-hard, a jerk, and a yo-yo. And you'll never scare me again, because even they see that you're the bad one. I'm the good one. *(He gets up and lies on the downstage bed to get away from her. She follows and sits next to him on that bed.)* You set my brother up to steal from you by not giving him a big enough Christmas bonus. You set up my punishing you when I withhold in sex because you punish me with your premature ejaculations. When that old man told you how long he could go with his wife, I knew you were a phoney. This looks like gloating, doesn't it, Nick? It's justice. Maybe after you realize that I'll be able to forgive

49

you and even love you again, if I can stand to look at your face. *(She gets up and walks toward the door.)* Now get back in there, because the only chance this marriage has is for me to take a good look at the rest of my hate.

NICK. *(Sits up slowly.)* My neck's killing me.

WENDY. Just your neck? By the time you've admitted what you've done to me, the children, my family, the society you live in and the world at large, there won't be any part of your body left that doesn't ache. Move it, twerp! *(He walks out the door looking like he wants to kill her. WENDY continues on her way out.)* I haven't had this much fun since you got your threatening finger caught in the toaster. Life is good. It's really good. *(She goes out laughing and closes the door behind her.)*

(Lights fade out.)

Scene Four

Lights fade up on the same room. It is night time and the room is dark. The door opens and NICK and WENDY enter. They both look haggard. They don't say a word to each other. He turns on the light, then they both sit down on the couch, stare blankly into space and think for a long moment.

WENDY. I have never been so depressed in my life.

NICK. Sadistic bastards.

WENDY. I don't know why I came. At first I thought you were the bully and I was the victim. Then I thought I was the bully and you were the victim. Now I see we're both victims.

NICK. And we paid those bastards $600 to find that out. Well, we weren't victims until we came here. They made us victims. That's how they make their money. They see two normal people walk in and they don't quit till they turn them into sickos. We gotta get out of here! I want my money back. I'm going to demand it. *(He gets up and rushes into the bathroom.)*

WENDY. They don't give refunds. They say they do but it's just a trick. To get it back, I hear they make you work airports signing up other sickos. Let's just sneak out quietly and forget the whole thing. I just want to go home, take a hot bath, get under the covers and die. I had so much to live for when I came here. Now there's nothing. Nothing but despair and....

51

NICK. *(Comes out of the bathroom with the suitcase and cosmetic case and he picks up the other suitcase from the foot of the downstage bed.)* Will you stop that? You're scaring me. *(Goes to the door with all the suitcases. He listens at the door.)* Shhh! There's somebody there. *(He opens the door slowly. They both peek out.)* Aha!

WENDY. It's only a chamber maid.

NICK. Yeah, but how do we know she isn't with them? *(He closes the door and he crosses to the patio area. WENDY follows.)* Let's go out to the patio, climb the fence, and get out of here. *(He opens the sliding glass doors and she follows him out onto the patio. He puts down the suitcases and looks around for a way to climb the fence.)*

WENDY. Nick, we can't leave like this. It's too upsetting and you'll hurt your bad neck climbing that.

NICK. *(Stands on a patio chair.)* I don't care. We need a rope with a hook.

WENDY. My friend, Joanie Cooper, snuck out and she hated herself for months.

NICK. Joanie Cooper has always hated herself.

WENDY. But she hated herself more, much more. Nick, we can't quit. We'll never hear the end of it from all our friends who graduated. Let's go back in there and show them we can take it.

NICK. *(Thinks for a moment, then comes back in beleagueredly and heads for the door.)* If that group leader calls me an asshole one more time, I'll go right for his throat. *(He exits.)*

WENDY. Life stinks. It really stinks. *(She exits and closes the door behind her.)*

(Lights fade out.)

Scene Five

Lights fade up. The same room. It is now morning. Bright sunlight shines in through the glass doors. The front door opens and NICK and WENDY come in dancing buoyantly. They're both singing a love song. *"You Stepped Out Of A Dream." They ballroom dance around the room. He dips her.

WENDY. Oh, Nick, this is the happiest I could ever remember being. The graduation ceremony was so elating. I could dance forever.

NICK. Champagne! We have to order champagne!

WENDY. Nickie, it's six o'clock in the morning. Room service isn't open.

NICK. Who needs champagne anyway? I'm high on life.

WENDY. We're drunk with life. *(They clink and drink from imaginary glasses. They look at each other for a moment, then kiss passionately.)*

WENDY. Oh, Nick, I love you.

NICK. I love you more than I've ever loved you before. *(He kisses her on the neck.)*

WENDY. *(She cries.)* This is the most touching experience of my life.

NICK. I'm so filled with love, I could have sex with you for a week.

*Note: Permission to produce *Bedrooms* does *not* include permission to use this song in production. This permission should be procured from the copyright owner.

WENDY. I love everyone in that auditorium.

NICK. *(He starts to cry.)* I love everyone and they love me.

WENDY. We love them and they love us.

NICK. And the leader — what a guy — I love him.

WENDY. I love him too. And the one who guarded the door who I called a fascist. What a cute guy.

NICK. Oh, boy.

WENDY. What?

NICK. Remember when we thought they were schmucks?

WENDY. Remember when we thought we were victims? That seems so ridiculous now. When I realize that life *IS*. It just *IS*.

NICK. Wow, isn't that some insight? Life *IS*. It's so simple but I never realized it before. Life *IS*.

WENDY. And so what? What about that insight? So what?

NICK. We've got a fourteen-year-old kid who smokes dope. So what? *(They both laugh hysterically.)*

WENDY. So what that your mother insults me?

NICK. And that your brother stole from me. Why should I let any of it make me crazy when I created it. And it is.

WENDY. And so what? *(They both laugh so hard that they fall onto the couch.)* Oh, Nick, when I take responsibility for everything and I see how little it all means, I don't see how I could ever fight with you again.

NICK. There's no good guys and no bad guys, so how could there be a fight?

WENDY. But didn't I always say that we didn't have

to fight?

NICK. No, honey, you always said we should fight to get it over with.

WENDY. Only when there was a fight going on and I felt we should bring it out in the open.

NICK. Yeah, but something inside me said that none of our fights were necessary, even when you started them.

WENDY. That's a judgement, Nick.

NICK. No it isn't.

WENDY. Nick, take responsibility for making a judgment about my starting fights.

NICK. *(Thinks for a moment.)* Alright. I'll take responsibility for possibly judging you, but you have to take responsibility for allowing it to make you feel like a victim.

WENDY. You take responsibility first.

NICK. No, you take it first. You made it into a conflict.

WENDY. This is ridiculous. We'll count to three and we'll both take responsibility together.

BOTH. One ... two ... three....

WENDY. I just took responsibility.

NICK. I didn't. So what? ... Get it? So what? It's no big deal. So what?

WENDY. That is not a "so what."

NICK. Everything is a "so what."

WENDY. Tricking your wife into taking responsibility and you're not taking it is not a "so what."

NICK. Wendy, I'm not going to fight with you no matter what you say.

WENDY. Nick, you're using the self-encounter technique to validate your refusing to apoligize.

NICK. So what? Get it? So what? Honey, nothing matters. It's all bullshit. That's the ultimate insight.

WENDY. *(She stands.)* You're making an ass out of yourself, Nick.

NICK. *(He stands.)* You just called me a name, Wendy.

WENDY. Take responsibility for what you just did, Nick.

NICK. Apologize for calling me a name.

WENDY. Go to hell.

NICK. How would you like a kick in the ass?

WENDY. How would you like my fist up your nose?

NICK. Bitch!

WENDY. Schmuck!

NICK. Whore!

WENDY. Shithead!

NICK. Woa! I stop. I take it back. I'm sorry. *(He sits back down on the couch.)*

WENDY. I take it back. I'm sorry too. *(She sits on the couch.)*

NICK. Whew! That was close.

WENDY. You still want to make love to me for a week?

NICK. Yeah ... but first let's rest. I'm a litle tired now.

WENDY. Me too. I want to nap for a minute. *(She leans her head on his shoulder.)*

NICK. Growth is exhausting. *(They close their eyes wearily and pass out.)*

(Lights fade out.)

MR. LEWIS
AND
MRS. WEXEL

MR. LEWIS AND MRS. WEXEL

Lights fade up. The set is a large new well-furnished South Florida condominium studio apartment. The entrance to the apartment is downstage left. Upstage left is a kitchen alcove. Just right of the alcove is a round dining table and four chairs. Downstage center is a couch, coffee table and two end chairs. Upstage right is an alcove for a daybed with cushions on it. Just left of the daybed alcove is a lounge chair and hassock. In the center of the upstage wall is a big bay window. Built into the stage right wall downstage of the daybed alcove is a bookcase/wetbar/TV/stereo unit. It is night time. The front door is opened with a key and two senior citizens, MR. LEWIS and MRS. WEXEL enter. MR. LEWIS turns on the light and closes the door.

MRS. WEXEL. *(studying the room)* Very nice. Very nice.

MR. LEWIS. It's got Hi-Fi stereo, Cable TV and a perfect view of the ocean. My children want only the best for me.

MRS. WEXEL. You must have wonderful children.

MR. LEWIS. Thank you.

MRS. WEXEL. You're welcome.... So, where's the fish?

MR. LEWIS. Come, look. Right over here. *(He leads her stage right to a small fish tank on one of the shelves of the bookcase.)*

MRS. WEXEL. Isn't that something? Just like in the aquarium.

MR. LEWIS. I thought you would be impressed. *(There's a long pause. Trying to be casual.)* So ... uh ... you want a drink?

MRS. WEXEL. No, I just wanted to see your apartment and the fish. *(She makes a move toward the door.)*

MR. LEWIS. Come on, have a drink.

MRS. WEXEL. I don't think it would look too good if the other women at the senior citizen's dance found out that I had a drink in the room of the peppiest looking eligible there.

MR. LEWIS. Who's going to tell? A drink is a good way to get to know each other.

MRS. WEXEL. In what area, Mr. Lewis? Because to me getting to know a person means feeling his spirituality and that we could do back at the dance. It's not that I don't trust you, Mr. Lewis, but we did only just meet. You know how people talk. If my children back in Chicago found out that I was in a strange man's condominium only three years after my late husband passed away, knock on wood, they'd think, God knows what.

MR. LEWIS. Look, I'm seventy-seven. My lovely wife was only laid to rest two years ago. I'm still in the state of shock myself. So, sit down and relax. *(She hesitates a moment.)* Sit! Sit!

MRS. WEXEL. *(Fans herself.)* It's a little warm in here.

MR. LEWIS. Let me take off your shawl. *(He helps her off with her shawl. She's wearing a sweater underneath. He blows on the material.)* Hmmm. Nice goods.

MRS. WEXEL. Are you in the clothing business?

MR. LEWIS. Don't you know who I am?

MRS. WEXEL. No. *(She sits in a chair.)*

MR. LEWIS. *(He sits on the couch.)* I told you my name was Leo Lewis and it meant nothing to you. But does the name L. Lewis and Son ring a bell?

MRS. WEXEL. No.

MR. LEWIS. I'm number one in low-priced misses coats, up to sixteen and half sizes. Here's my card.

MRS. WEXEL. You gave me one at the dance.

MR. LEWIS. Have another. I got plenty. Then the next time you pass a J.C. Penney, look in the window. That's my coat with the gold buttons, the frog epilets and the monk's hood with the tassels.

MRS. WEXEL. That's your coat? *(He nods.)* Stunning. You're a very talented designer.

MR. LEWIS. What designer? It's a Dior from Paris. I copied it down. $49.95. That coat was a dud till I added the shoulder braids and the belt with the whistle and the sword.

MRS. WEXEL. Well, sure sometimes you make up in volume what you lack in taste.

MR. LEWIS. So, what can I get you to drink? *(He walks to the bar.)*

MRS. WEXEL. Alright, I'll have a grasshopper.

MR. LEWIS. I don't know how to make that. If you want something fancy, the only thing I can give you is some coconut brandy with a piece of banana.

MRS. WEXEL. *(She thinks about it.)* Okay, but put a little cream and sugar in it. *(He begins mixing her a drink.)* So, what do you think of the types they get at this retirement community, with the wigs and the face lifts and the false lashes? Me, I comb my hair. I wash my face. I put on a dress and that's it.

MRS. LEWIS. Let me tell you something, Mrs. Wexel. It's refreshing to be with you. You stood out tonight like a sore thumb. *(He turns on the phonograph. Soft music plays. He hands her a drink and sits next to her on the couch.)*

MRS. WEXEL. *(Takes a sip.)* Mmmm. Very tasty.

MR. LEWIS. *(There's an awkward silence as he inches toward her.)* So, you're a widow three years?

MRS. WEXEL. That's right.

MR. LEWIS. *(another pause)* How long were you married?

MRS. WEXEL. Forty-eight years.

MR. LEWIS. Were you compatible?

MRS. WEXEL. *(sighs)* He was happy, that's the main thing.

MR. LEWIS. *(another pause)* How important do you think sex is in marriage?

MRS. WEXEL. *(Thinks for a long moment.)* Two-fifths.

MR. LEWIS. I was married fifty-one years to a wonderful woman. I miss her very much. You want to dance?

MRS. WEXEL. *(Thinks about it.)* Okay, but don't twirl me. I get dizzy. *(They begin dancing the cha-cha.)*

MR. LEWIS. *(After a short while, he pulls her close to him and whispers in her ear.)* What do you say we finish this dance under the sheets?

MRS. WEXEL. *(Stops dancing and sinks down wearily on the couch.)* Oy!

MR. LEWIS. *(Sits next to her and whispers in her ear again.)* Don't worry. I'll let you stay the whole night.

MRS. WEXEL. Oy! You must be kidding. This isn't

really happening. It's an obscene phone call in person.

MR. LEWIS. Look, we don't even have to move to the bed. The couch opens up. *(He kisses her shoulder excitedly.)* It'll just take a minute of your time.

MRS. WEXEL. *(Tries to get away from his clutches.)* Please keep away from me. I have a heart condition.

MR. LEWIS. *(excitedly)* Look, kiss me. You can always change your mind in the middle. Come on, you'll like it. You could do a lot worse. Come on, let's get in the nude, *(He grabs her and she pushes his shoulder and gets free.)* Hey, easy! I've got bursitis! *(He rubs his shoulder.)*

MRS. WEXEL. Where's my shawl? I'm leaving!

MR. LEWIS. Come on. Stop putting on airs. You're looking for the same thing as I am. How can you go three years without a thrill. You're only human.

MRS. WEXEL. *(tearfully)* I'm human. Thank you very much. That's the first nice thing you've said to me. That and the sore thumb. Not, I'm loveable. Not, I have a wonderful personality. Not, I'm charming. I'm just human.

MR. LEWIS. Well, of course. Those other things go without saying. Otherwise why would I invite you to my apartment? Don't forget there are maybe two women to every man at that dance, but it was you I chose to have a hot time with.

MRS. WEXEL. *(with suffering)* Two women to every man. You're all the same. You know the odds. You make a study of them and then you throw it in our faces because we're women and we're still alive and our husbands died before us and you know we feel guilty. Well, let me tell you something, Mr. Lewis. I'm not guilty. He was the guilty one when he was alive and the guilty one when he died. I warned him. I said, "Harry, slow down," but he wouldn't listen to me. He chased the chippies till the end. I went to claim his body in a motel in Miami. He checked in with some chippie in the afternoon and by the middle of the night he was gone. I'll never forget the expression on his face when I saw him. He was dead, but he had this guilty look about him and you want to hear my autopsy report .... It was the guilt and not the chippie that killed him. He was the guilty one. Not me.

MR. LEWIS. *(There's a long pause.)* So, what's it gonna be?

MRS. WEXEL. What's it gonna be? Give me my shawl! That's what it's gonna be! Where's my shawl? *(She starts looking for her shawl in ridiculous places like under the couch, behind a chair.)*

MR. LEWIS. *(trying to grab her)* What's your hurry? Give me a chance to show you what I can do. Let me give you a free sample. No obligations.

MRS. WEXEL. *(pulling herself free)* You want an orgy? Find yourself a horse of another color!

MR. LEWIS. Look, maybe I rushed you a little. You're sensitive. You want me to start slowly. Let me take your hand. Here. *(He takes her hand gently.)* I'll hold it. I'll pat it. I'll stroke it. I'll kiss it. *(He starts kissing her hand. Then her arm and her neck.)*

MRS. WEXEL. Let go of me, or I'll scream!

MR. LEWIS. Can I help it if you turn me on? *(He tries to kiss her.)*

MRS. WEXEL. *(screaming)* Help! Rape! Police! Rape! Help!

MR. LEWIS. *(He lets her go.)* Okay, let's forget it. If that's how you feel about it, I'm sorry I bothered you.

MRS. WEXEL. *(Pulls herself together.)* Thank you.

MR. LEWIS. *(very hurt)* I don't need this aggravation. I'll take you back to the dance.

MRS. WEXEL. I would appreciate that.

MR. LEWIS. There's no hard feelings, but you started it. You led me on.

MRS. WEXEL. I led you on?

MR. LEWIS. What kind of a woman goes to a public dancing place and doesn't wear a girdle?

MRS. WEXEL. *(She slaps his face.)* Don't talk fresh to me.... No girdle. That's how much you know. I am wearing a girdle, but without the bones. *(She lifts her dress absentmindedly to show her girdle.)*

MR. LEWIS. *(He sees her girdle and gets excited and tries to grab her.)* One hug! Just one hug! *(He grabs her.)*

MRS. WEXEL. *(She pulls away from him.)* You tricked me. I'm mad at you. You misrepresented yourself. You ingratiated yourself to me about your business and your sensitivity to fish. Now I see you're a phoney. I don't even think you're Jewish.

MR. LEWIS. You should talk. I'm a phoney? You're a double phoney. Who did you think would invite you up to his apartment, but a swinger? You dance sexy with me. You lead me to believe you're not wearing a girdle. From the minute you met me you knew what I had in mind. You knew the jig was up. You're no virgin. So, let me ask you something. What are you doing standing here listening to my explanation? How come you didn't leave ten minutes ago? Huh? Huh? *(trying to be George Raft)* I'll tell you why. Because I turn you on, baby. You act aloof and superior and you talk about wanting to know me spiritually. But, I got your number, sister. What you really want is my goods.

MRS. WEXEL. I want your goods? Mishugena!! What I want is companionship, warmth, friendship, a rapport, kindness, respect, admiration, affection. You know how long I'm looking for these things? 75 years. And you think just because you can't give me them I'm not going to find those things? You think I'm not entitled to those things in this life because I'm not so lovable and what I should settle for instead is your goods? *(She thinks about it and then plops down on the couch.)* Alright, let's have them! I'll try it. What'll it cost me?

MR. LEWIS. What?

MRS. WEXEL. So, go ahead. Rape me. I promise I won't move a muscle. I'll just lie there quiet like a mouse and make out my shopping list for the week and maybe have a good time.

MR. LEWIS. You mean it?

MRS. WEXEL. Why not? I'll probably never see you again anyway and lonely I can always be. It's nothing special. So, let me see what one night of degenerate fruit is like.

MR. LEWIS. You won't be sorry. *(He starts pulling off his jacket and tie like a young school boy.)*

MRS. WEXEL. *(She starts unbuttoning her sweater very delicately, revealing still another sweater underneath. She starts unbuttoning that sweater and then begins taking off her ankle-strap shoes. Over the previous business.)* You know I've always been too sexy looking for my own good. But, I'll tell you the truth. I never felt a thing in that department. But I look around me, the whole world is making such a federal case about sex ... for it, against it, in the schools, picketing in the streets, in the clothes, in the music. Maybe I missed out on the fabulous parts of the experience. Maybe I'm not so smart or why would I be so frigid? (*MR. LEWIS begins taking his pants off frantically, not listening to a thing she's been saying. He tries to get his pants off over his shoes. He's wearing long underwear. Finally, he gets his pants and shoes off. When MRS. WEXEL sees his long underwear, she puts her hands over her eyes, but sneaks a peek. MR. LEWIS stands up straight and begins to go toward her in a virile stride, then suddenly he gets dizzy and sits down and begins to rub his forehead.*) What's the matter?

MR. LEWIS. I don't feel so good. I think it was that lamb with pineapple sauce I had for dinner. It feels like it's laying on my chest.

MRS. WEXEL. Maybe it's your gall bladder.

MR. LEWIS. No, I had that taken out.

MRS. WEXEL. How's your kidneys?

MR. LEWIS. Fine. How's yours?

MRS. WEXEL. Pretty good. How are your joints? You said you have bursitis?

MR. LEWIS. Once in awhile it acts up. A little lumbago, a little arthritis, a little asthma. Otherwise, I'm a hundred percent.

MRS. WEXEL. You're lucky, you're an ox like me. I've got an enlarged heart. Once in awhile my pressure goes up. I have palpitations. I can't breathe. A few sharp pains here and there, but knock on wood, nothing serious. How do you sleep at night?

MR. LEWIS. Four hours, maybe.

MRS. WEXEL. That's two more than me. Did you ever get a pain that starts in your head and goes past the side of your nose and into your throat so you can't swallow and it shoots down your whole side to your knee?

MR. LEWIS. Many times. But, did your foot ever swell up so that you have to walk leaning to the other side so that the extra weight causes your hip to get stiff, sending a numbness through your spine and a sharp pain up your neck pinching the nerve in your shoulder?

MRS. WEXEL. You get that? Tsk, tsk, tsk. Sometimes I have a throb under my arm and it works it's way across my chest and gives me a spasm in my arm, causing me to lose the use of my thumb.

MR. LEWIS. I never heard of such a thing in my life. *(There's a pause.)* But did you ever hear of this? You move your head a certain way and your cheek feels like it's falling so that you lift your head up fast and you get dizzy and you look down fast and you get nauseous? That's what I got now.

MRS. WEXEL. Is that so? You know something? The moment I laid eyes on you tonight I didn't like the way you looked.

MR. LEWIS. I looked bad?

MRS. WEXEL. Just tired, very tired. You had this "I gotta live it up" expression in your eyes, but the rest of you looked like it wanted to sit down and think it over.

MR. LEWIS. How could I be tired? I'm on vacation here. The whole winter. All I do is sleep and eat.

MRS. WEXEL. And what do you do when you're not on

vacation here?

MR. LEWIS. I walk in the park, I read the paper, I take a bath, and that's all. And once a week I go in my place and pick up my check from my son. Why should that make me tired?

MRS. WEXEL. *(Sighs knowingly.)* You struggle your whole life to build up a business. And what's more tiring than to sit in the park, read a paper, take a bath and pick up a check from your son? You know how much that check weighs, Mr. Lewis? Seventy-seven years.

MR. LEWIS. *(Thinks about it. On the verge of tears.)* You know! You know! I'm finished. It's all over for me. I'm a walking dead man.

MRS. WEXEL. Lay down. Put your feet up. *(She lifts his feet on the couch and puts a throw over him.)* Cry, Leo, cry. It's good for you. That's what you really needed. Not that other business.

MR. LEWIS. They put me here. They keep putting me in fancy places like this since my wife died. My son and my daughter-in-law. Who needs it? What am I doing surrounded by bamboo furniture? My wife would have liked it. She would have put plastic slipcovers over the bamboo. For forty-two years she had a plastic slipcover over me. Your sex life sounds like a pornographic movie next to mine. I got nothing. Nothing. *(He looks up to heaven.)* So why can't I go a little crazy now, Bertha? Why? *(He pauses.)* It's just like her to give me the silent treatment.

MRS. WEXEL. So let her. What do you care? You're entitled. *(She looks up to heaven.)* That goes for me too, Bertha. *(to MR. LEWIS)* Move over a little. Give me some room. *(He does. She lays down beside him and rests her head on his chest.)*

MR. LEWIS. *(after a pause)* I don't know if I feel so sexy anymore. Maybe it was just nervousness.

MRS. WEXEL. Don't worry about it.

MR. LEWIS. No, look, my word is my bond. Just let me close my eyes and rest a little and maybe later, or tomorrow morning first thing, we'll do a little something.

MRS. WEXEL. Sure, Leo, sure. *(He closes his eyes.)* Look, I waited this long. *(She smiles and pats his stomach.)*

(Lights fade out.)

THE OFFICE PLAYS
Two full length plays by Adam Bock

THE RECEPTIONIST
Comedy / 2m, 2f / Interior
At the start of a typical day in the Northeast Office, Beverly deals effortlessly with ringing phones and her colleague's romantic troubles. But the appearance of a charming rep from the Central Office disrupts the friendly routine. And as the true nature of the company's business becomes apparent, The Receptionist raises disquieting, provocative questions about the consequences of complicity with evil.

"...Mr. Bock's poisoned Post-it note of a play."
- New York Times

"Bock's intense initial focus on the routine goes to the heart of *The Receptionist's* pointed, painfully timely allegory... elliptical, provocative play..."
- Time Out New York

THE THUGS
Comedy / 2m, 6f / Interior
The Obie Award winning dark comedy about work, thunder and the mysterious things that are happening on the 9th floor of a big law firm. When a group of temps try to discover the secrets that lurk in the hidden crevices of their workplace, they realize they would rather believe in gossip and rumors than face dangerous realities.

"Bock starts you off giggling, but leaves you with a chill."
- Time Out New York

"... a delightfully paranoid little nightmare that is both more chillingly realistic and pointedly absurd than anything John Grisham ever dreamed up."
- New York Times

SAMUELFRENCH.COM

Breinigsville, PA USA
29 December 2010
252409BV00005B/5/P